Karen's Secret

Look for these
and other books about Karen
in the
Baby-sitters Little Sister series:

Little Sister

Karen's Secret
Ann M. Martin

Illustrations by Susan Tang

A
LITTLE APPLE
PAPERBACK

SCHOLASTIC INC.
New York Toronto London Auckland Sydney

If you purchased this book without a cover, you should be aware that this book is stolen property. It was reported as "unsold and destroyed" to the publisher, and neither the author nor the publisher has received any payment for this "stripped book."

No part of this publication may be reproduced in whole or in part, or stored in a retrieval system, or transmitted in any form or by any means, electronic, mechanical, photocopying, recording, or otherwise, without written permission of the publisher. For information regarding permission, write to Scholastic Inc., 730 Broadway, New York, NY 10003.

ISBN 0-590-45648-2

Copyright © 1992 by Ann M. Martin. All rights reserved. Published by Scholastic Inc. APPLE PAPERBACKS and BABY-SITTERS LITTLE SISTER are registered trademarks of Scholastic Inc.

12 11 10 9 8 7 6 5   6 7/9

Printed in the U.S.A.   40

First Scholastic printing, November 1992

The author gratefully acknowledges
Stephanie Calmenson
for her help
with this book.

The Big Sister

"I know!" I cried. "If the baby is a boy, you should name him George Washington Dawes!"

I was in my room with my friend, Nancy Dawes. I was helping her think of a name for her new baby brother or sister.

"That is perfect!" Nancy giggled. "Mommy and Daddy will love it!"

"And if it is a girl, you can name her Karen Brewer the Second, after me," I said.

Well, now you know my name. It is Karen Brewer. I will tell you a few more important things about myself. I am seven years old. I have blonde hair, blue eyes, and some freckles. I wear glasses. I have two pairs. Blue for reading. Pink for other things.

Nancy is one of my two best friends. She lives next door to Mommy's house. (Hannie Papadakis is my other best friend. She lives across the street and one house down from Daddy.)

Nancy is going to become a big sister in a couple of months. It is gigundoly exciting. I am a big sister already. I have a little brother, Andrew. He is four going on five. My adopted sister, Emily Michelle, is two and a half.

"I still think Matthew is a great name for a boy. And Jilly for a girl," said Nancy.

"Just don't name anyone Biff Bartholomew or April May," I said. Those were the first names Nancy liked. She has changed her mind a zillion times since her mommy and daddy said she could name the baby.

"Maybe I should not give the baby such a great name, anyway," said Nancy.

"Why not?" I asked.

"Well, I am a little bit scared that Mommy and Daddy will like the baby better than me. Babies are cute," said Nancy. "Were you scared when Andrew and Emily Michelle came?"

"I don't remember. I was only three when Andrew was born. That was a long time ago. And Emily Michelle was adopted and she lives with Daddy. That is different," I explained.

"What if the baby is really smart? Smarter than me. Or great at sports. Or a great actor. What if it does *everything* better than me?" said Nancy.

"Don't worry. Being a big sister is going to be fun," I said.

"Maybe," said Nancy. "But I am not going to take any chances. I am going to make sure that Mommy and Daddy love me no matter how wonderful the baby is. From now on I am going to be so, so good.

I will start by helping around the house."

"And when the baby comes, you can help take care of it. That will really make them love you. We can practice on Hyacynthia," I suggested. (Hyacynthia is the special baby doll Nancy and I share.)

"Good idea," said Nancy. "I think I hear her crying."

Nancy picked up Hyacynthia. She was singing a lullaby when Andrew raced into my room. He did not knock first.

"You are supposed to knock!" I yelled.

"I forgot," Andrew replied. "Mommy is making cookies. She said we can help."

"We will help you eat them later. We are busy now," I said.

"The cookies will be all gone by the time you get there. I am a cookie monster!" Andrew ran around the room flapping his arms. Then he flew out the door.

Nancy had a funny look on her face.

"Don't worry," I told her again. "Being a big sister will be fun. Really."

I do not think Nancy believed me.

Big Sister, Little Sister

I am a big sister. I am a little sister. I have a big house. I have a little house. Do you want to know why? I will tell you.

A long time ago, Mommy, Daddy, Andrew, and I lived together in one big house here in Stoneybrook, Connecticut. I was a big sister with one little brother. I liked that just fine. But Mommy and Daddy were not happy. They loved Andrew and me. But they decided they did not love each other enough to live together anymore. So they got divorced.

Mommy moved with Andrew and me to a little house. (It is not too far from Daddy's house.) Then Mommy met Seth Engle. They got married. Now Seth is my stepfather. He is very nice. So are Midgie, his dog, and Rocky, his cat.

We all live together in the little house. At least, that is where Andrew and I live most of the time. Oh, I forgot to tell you about Emily Junior. She is my very own pet rat. She lives with us, too.

After the divorce Daddy stayed at the big house. (He grew up there.) Then he met Elizabeth Thomas. They got married. Now Elizabeth is my stepmother. She has four children. They are my stepbrothers and stepsister. They are all older than me. (That is how I got to be a little sister.) I will tell you about them. David Michael is seven, but an older seven than me. Sam and Charlie are so old they are in high school. Kristy is thirteen. She is one of my favorite people in the whole world. (She is a wonderful baby-sitter, too.)

Then Emily Michelle joined the family. I got to be a big sister all over again. I told you that Emily Michelle is two and a half. And that she is adopted. But I did not tell you that she came from a faraway place called Vietnam. Mostly I like Emily Michelle a lot. That is why I named my rat after her.

There is one more person at the big house. Nannie. She is Elizabeth's mother. That makes her my stepgrandmother. She helps take care of Emily Michelle when Daddy and Elizabeth are at work and everyone else is at school.

There are lots of pets at the big house, too. Shannon is David Michael's Bernese mountain dog puppy. Boo-Boo is Daddy's crabby cat. Crystal Light the Second is my goldfish. And Goldfishie is Andrew's fish.

Andrew and I live at the big house every other weekend, on some holidays and vacations, and for two weeks during the summer.

I have special names for Andrew and me.

7

I call us Andrew Two-Two and Karen Two-Two. (I thought of those names after my teacher, Ms. Colman, read us a book called *Jacob Two-Two Meets the Hooded Fang*.) Andrew and I are Two-Twos because we have two of lots of different things. Two mommies and two daddies, two cats and two dogs, and even two houses. Plus, we have two sets of clothes. (At the big house and the little house. That is so we do not have to carry much when we go back and forth between our houses.) We have toys and books at each house. I have two bicycles. Andrew has two tricycles. I have two stuffed cats: Moosie lives at the big house. Goosie lives at the little house. I even have two pieces of Tickly, my special blue blanket. (I had to rip Tickly in half because I kept leaving Tickly at one house or the other. I need Tickly to go to sleep.)

Well, anyway, now you know how I got to be a big sister two times. And a little sister four times. And you know how I became a two-two.

Telephone

Rain, rain, go away! Come again another day!

"Class, it is raining too hard to go outside. So we will have our recess indoors," said Ms. Colman.

Boo. I like going out at recess. I *need* to go out at recess. Ms. Colman says I have a lot of energy. She says it is good for me to run around. Also, I get to use my outdoor voice at recess. (That is my loud voice.)

Ms. Colman was writing at the blackboard. She was writing the names of games. Seven-up. Twenty Questions. Telephone. Recess was going to be fun after all. I love second grade! I love Ms. Colman!

"Raise your hand if you would like to play Seven-up," said Ms. Colman. "Twenty Questions? Telephone?"

"Ring! Ring!" I shouted.

"Indoor voice, please, Karen," said Ms. Colman.

"But it is recess," I explained.

"We are still indoors, and I will still get a headache if you shout," Ms. Colman replied.

I did not want to give Ms. Colman a headache. So I raised my hand. I wiggled my fingers. "Ring, ring!" I said in a very high — but not very loud — voice.

We divided into groups. I will tell you who was in my group for Telephone. Hannie and Nancy. (We are the Three Musketeers. We like to do everything together.) Ricky Torres. (He is my pretend husband. We both sit in the front row because we wear glasses.) Natalie Springer. (She sits up front and wears glasses, too.) Bobby Gi-

10

anelli. (Sometimes he is a bully.) Pamela Harding. (Too bad. She is my best enemy.) Leslie Morris and Jannie Gilbert. (They are Pamela's friends.)

Here is how you play Telephone. Everyone stands in a line. Whoever goes first whispers something to the next person. The next person whispers it to the next, and so on. The last person says the sentence out loud. And you know what? The sentence is almost never the same as when it started. It gets mixed up along the way.

Ms. Colman wrote a sentence on a piece of paper. She handed it to Hannie. Hannie was going to go first. We had picked numbers from a shoe box on Ms. Colman's desk. I was number seven. That was a good number. By the time the sentence got to me, it would be extra silly.

Psst-psst-psst-psst. I could hear Hannie's voice. She was whispering to Ricky. But I could not hear the words.

Psst-psst-psst-psst. Ricky whispered to Nancy. Nancy whispered to Natalie. Na-

11

talie whispered to Pamela. Pamela whispered to Bobby.

Finally it was my turn. Bobby whispered the secret sentence to me. *Psst-psst-psst-psst.*

"Amy's name is Harry and her hubby's name is Sal!" I shouted.

Oops.

"Ka-ren!" cried Jannie. "You were not supposed to say the sentence out loud. You were supposed to whisper it to *me*."

"Now I don't get a turn," moaned Leslie.

"Blarin' Karen strikes again," said Bobby. "The sentence was supposed to be a secret till the end. But Blarin' Karen can't keep a secret."

"I am very sorry I ruined the game. But you do not have to call me names," I shouted.

Everyone in the room turned to look at me and my group.

"Um, Ms. Colman," I said in my best indoor voice. "May we have another sentence please?"

Natalie's Secret

"See you tomorrow!" I called to Nancy, when Mrs. Dawes came to pick her up.

Nancy and I usually ride home from school together. But Mrs. Dawes was going to the obstetrician. (That's the special doctor for women who are going to have babies.) Nancy was going with her mother.

"See you tomorrow!" I called to Hannie, when her mother arrived.

" 'Bye, Ricky!" I called.

" 'Bye, Terri and Tammy!" I said. (Terri and Tammy are twins.)

Soon Natalie and I were the only ones left. We were waiting for our mommies to come. Natalie kept pulling up her socks. When she was not pulling up her socks, she was chewing on her nails. I could tell she was upset.

"What's wrong?" I asked.

"Nothing," replied Natalie.

"Are you sure? You do not look very happy," I said.

"It's a secret," said Natalie.

"You can tell *me* your secret!" I tried not to sound too excited. But it was hard. Secrets are cool.

Natalie shook her head. "I do not think I want to tell you," she said. "I do not think it would be a secret anymore if I did."

"I won't tell anyone. I promise," I replied.

"I do not think so," said Natalie.

"Cross my heart and hope to die!"

"No," said Natalie.

"I know I told the Telephone secret. But that was different. It was a game. I would never tell anyone's real and true secret," I promised.

"Well," said Natalie.

"Puh-lease!" I begged.

Natalie took a deep breath. Hurray! She was going to tell me her secret. She leaned over and whispered in my ear.

"*Psst-psst-psst-psst.*"

"What?" I said. "I couldn't understand you."

"*Psst-psst-psst-psst,*" Natalie repeated.

"What about a test? Can't you just say it out loud?" I asked. "No one else is here."

Natalie looked around. Then she said, "The principal says I have to take a special test. I don't know what the test is for. Maybe it is because I'm dumb. Maybe they are going to put me in another class."

Poor Natalie. This was gigundoly sad news. I wanted to make her feel better.

"Maybe it is a test for something good," I said.

"Like what?" asked Natalie.

"Like . . . like . . . um," I said. I always have good ideas. But my mind was blank. What kind of test could be good? I thought hard. But I could not think of a single one.

"Remember your promise," said Natalie. "I do not want the rest of the kids to know about this."

"I won't tell anyone," I said. "Scout's honor."

"But you are not a scout," said Natalie.

"Then Karen Brewer's honor," I said. "That is just as good."

Honk! Honk! Our mommies arrived at the exact same time.

I waved good-bye with one hand. I covered my mouth with the other. I wanted to show Natalie what a good secret-keeper I was going to be.

Heartbeat

*D**ing, dong!*

I was upstairs in my room at the little house when the doorbell rang.

"I hope it is for us," I said to Goosie.

Guess what. It *was* for us. It was Nancy.

"Hi, Karen. I just got back from going to the doctor with Mommy. It was amazing," said Nancy.

I just love amazing stories. "Tell me what happened," I said.

"Well, first the doctor weighed Mommy. Then she listened to the baby's heartbeat with a stethoscope. The doctor let me and Mommy listen, too. It was neat," said Nancy.

"What did it sound like?" I asked. I wanted to know everything — in case I decided to be a mother some day.

"It sounded kind of like this: *glub-glub, glub-glub*," said Nancy.

"Cool!" I said. "What else?"

"I got to see a picture of the baby on a screen. I saw its head. And I saw its fingers and toes. There is a *real* baby in there," said Nancy.

"It won't be in there long," I said. "It is going to be out here pretty soon."

"Maybe the baby likes being in there. Maybe it will decide to stay," said Nancy.

"I do not think your mommy will let it," I replied.

"When the baby comes, everyone will be very busy. They will forget all about me," said Nancy sadly. "I better start doing good deeds around the house very soon. I have to be the best, most helpful daughter ever.

Maybe then they won't forget me."

"I will do good deeds with you!" I offered. "Let's make a list right now." I found a purple pencil and a piece of paper.

"This is great!" said Nancy. "The first thing I will do is clean my room. Mommy and Daddy will like that."

That did not sound like much fun to me, but I wrote it down. I decided to let Nancy do that herself.

"We can fluff up all the pillows in the house," I said. "Then your mommy will be comfortable when she sits down."

"Good idea," said Nancy. "And I can dust. That way Mommy won't sneeze. I think maybe it hurts her tummy when she sneezes."

I added "Fluff the pillows" and "Dust the house" to the list.

"There are always piles of laundry to be folded," said Nancy.

"I am not very good at folding," I told her.

"Me neither. We can remind Daddy to

do it," said Nancy. "That is his job."

"That will be very helpful," I said. I wrote it down.

"Karen! It's time for dinner," called Mommy.

"I guess I better go," said Nancy. "I'm going to start doing these good deeds as soon as I get home."

I gave Nancy the list. She folded it and put it in her pocket. When she was gone, I started feeling proud.

"Hey, Goosie, listen to this," I said. "I knew Natalie's secret. But I did not tell it to Nancy. That is pretty good."

I could tell Goosie wanted to say something to me. I held him up to my ear.

"What? You want me to tell the secret to you? No way," I said. "Natalie's secret is safe with me."

Telling Nancy

It was Wednesday morning. I had finished copying our new spelling words. (I am very good at spelling, by the way.)

I turned around to wave to Nancy. She sits in the back row with Hannie. Only Hannie was home with a cold.

"If you have finished copying the words, Karen, you may read until the others are ready," said Ms. Colman.

Oh, good, I thought. I took out my book. It was called *The Witches*, by Roald Dahl. This was a very good book for me to read.

That is because a witch lives next door to Daddy's house. Her name is Morbidda Destiny and . . .

"Attention, students. Will Natalie Springer please report to the nurse's office?"

Wow! A special announcement had come over the P.A. system for Natalie. I knew Natalie's test was today. But I did not know it was going to be in the nurse's office. Natalie looked upset. I do not think she knew it was going to be in the nurse's office either.

Uh-oh. What kind of test could they give in the nurse's office? A medical test. That's what kind. Maybe Natalie was sick.

After she left, I tried to read my book. I read the same page about six times. I could not keep my mind on the words. All I could think about was Natalie. Poor, poor Natalie.

"Karen? Are you listening?" said Ms. Colman. "I asked you please to put away your book and get ready for our math lesson."

24

"Sorry," I said. I tried to think about math. But instead of looking at the blackboard, I kept looking at the door. I wanted Natalie to come back. But she did not come back to the room all morning. By lunchtime, I felt like crying.

"Natalie!" I called, when my classmates and I reached the cafeteria. She was sitting at a table by herself. She looked even more upset than before.

"What happened?" I asked. "What kind of test was it?"

"I do not want to talk about it," said Natalie.

"Come on," I said. "You can tell me."

Natalie shook her head. She would not say another word.

I felt so bad, I could hardly eat my lunch. I managed to take one little bite. Then another. And another. Before I knew it, my sandwich was gone. And my milk too. Nancy and I ran outside.

I did not want to tell. Really I did not. But I knew if I did not tell Natalie's secret

to someone, I would explode. All over the school yard. I decided I could tell Nancy. That was just one person. And she was a Musketeer. A Musketeer would know how to keep a secret.

"Hey, Nancy," I said. "I have something important to tell you. But it is a secret and you cannot tell anyone else. Okay?"

"I can keep a secret," said Nancy. "What is it?"

I told Nancy about Natalie and her test. I told her how scared Natalie was.

"Then she got called to the nurse's office," I said. "She must be really sick. But remember, you can't tell anyone."

"I won't," said Nancy. "I promise."

"Thanks," I said. "I knew I could count on you."

What Is Wrong
with Natalie?

"*Attention, students. Will Natalie Springer please report to the nurse's office?*"

Oh, no! Not again. It was Monday morning. Natalie pulled up her socks and hurried out the door.

I waved good-bye. Then I turned to give Nancy an Important Look. She did not see me. She was whispering something to Hannie. They both looked very serious.

"All right, class," said Ms. Colman. "We are going to practice counting by twos up to one hundred. Karen, will you begin?"

"Two . . ." I said. Then I added, "Four! That would be Natalie's number."

"Thank you, Karen," said Ms. Colman. "Ricky, please continue."

"Six," said Ricky. (He is a very smart husband.)

We went around and around the room until we reached one hundred. Natalie was gone the whole time.

The same thing happened on Wednesday. An announcement came over the P.A. system for Natalie Springer. I turned to Nancy. She looked worried. So did Hannie. You know what? The whole back row — Nancy, Hannie, Hank Reubens, and Jannie Gilbert — looked worried.

Natalie was called out again on Friday. When I turned around to look at Nancy, I saw that half the class looked worried. They must have noticed that Natalie was being called out a lot. Something was wrong with Natalie. What could it be?

I decided to talk to Nancy at recess. She was standing around with Hannie.

"Um, excuse me, Hannie," I said. "Can I talk to Nancy for a minute?"

"If it's about Natalie," said Nancy, "we can talk in front of Hannie. I told her the secret. But she is the only person I told."

I did not mind that Nancy told Hannie. After all, Hannie is a Musketeer. We do not want to keep secrets from each other.

"What is wrong with Natalie?" I asked.

"Well, she does wear glasses. Do you think she is going blind?" asked Hannie.

"That is silly. *Lots* of people wear glasses. And they don't go blind," I said.

"Natalie is clumsy. Maybe the nurse is trying to find out why," said Nancy.

"She wouldn't be called out four times just for being clumsy," I said.

"I hope it's not termittal!" cried Hannie.

"You mean terminal," said Nancy. "It could not be. That would be just too awful!"

"We have to be super nice to Natalie now," I said. "And remember. No one is supposed to know she is going for tests. We have to keep it a secret."

The Good Deed Doers

"See you later, Mommy!" I called. It was a little-house Saturday. I was going over to Nancy's. I had promised to help her do good deeds.

"Hi, Karen!" said Nancy. "I have already cleaned my room and fluffed the pillows. I left a note for Daddy to fold the laundry. I think he is doing that now."

"Great," I replied.

Just then, Pokey raced out from under a chair. Pokey is Nancy's kitten. He darted up to me and rubbed against my leg.

"Oh, Pokey. You are so cute. And you love me so much, don't you?"

"Come on, Karen," said Nancy. "We have to get to work."

"I'm ready," I said. I ran my finger across the dining room table. I have seen Mommy do that at our house. "Tsk, tsk," I said, just the way she does. "Very dusty. We better get busy."

We dusted the entire house. We emptied the wastebaskets.

Mrs. Dawes came out of her study. She found us hard at work.

"This is awfully nice of you, girls," she said. "But wouldn't you rather go out and ride your bicycles? The weather is beautiful."

"Not today, Mommy," replied Nancy.

Mrs. Dawes went back to work. And so did we. We tied together all the old newspapers we could find. By the time we finished, the inside of the Dawes' house looked gigundoly clean.

"What now?" I asked.

"I heard Daddy say he was going to rake the leaves tomorrow morning," said Nancy.

"Let's go! To the leaves!" I said.

"To the leaves!" repeated Nancy.

Raking leaves was a fun job. We made a big pile. Then we jumped in. Of course we had to rake them all over again. But by the end of the afternoon, the lawn was clean and green.

"Nancy! Karen!" called Mrs. Dawes. "Would you like some cocoa and cookies?"

"Sure!" we said.

The cookies were peanut butter with raisins. They were Mrs. Dawes's specialty.

Mr. Dawes was taking a cocoa and cookie break, too.

"Thank you for raking the leaves, girls," he said. "You have been working very hard today. You usually do not work on Saturdays. Is there anything you want to talk to us about?"

"No, Daddy. I cannot think of anything," said Nancy.

"The house looks just lovely," said Mrs. Dawes. "But are you sure nothing is wrong? Did something happen at school?"

"Not a thing," I said.

"If anything is bothering you, remember you can always come to us," said Mr. Dawes.

"Thank you, Daddy," said Nancy.

"Thank you for the snack, Mrs. Dawes," I said. "It was very delicious. But now we have to get back to work. Is there anything special you would like done?"

Mr. and Mrs. Dawes just shook their heads.

"Okay!" I said. "We'll surprise you."

Nancy and I went down to the basement. We were sure we would find plenty of good deeds to do there.

Speech Lessons

On Monday morning Ms. Colman said, "We are going to begin a new science unit today. We will start by reading *The Magic School Bus Lost in the Solar System.*"

"Yea!" I cried. So did the rest of the class. The Magic School Bus books are neat. They are about this really smart teacher named Ms. Frizzle. (She's as smart as Ms. Colman.) She wears funny dresses. And she takes her class on amazing trips.

"Will the Magic School Bus go to Mars?" I asked.

"We'll see," said Ms. Colman. "As soon as everyone settles down, I will begin."

Ms. Colman read two sentences. Then Natalie was called to the nurse's office.

I could see that Natalie did not want to go. She did not stop to pull up her socks. She did not hurry out of the room. She kind of shuffled through the door.

I could not stand it anymore. I had to find out what was going on. I was going to find out as soon as I could.

Natalie was gone a whole half hour again. When she came back, Ms. Colman told her she could borrow the Magic School Bus book overnight.

"Thank you," mumbled Natalie. But she did not smile.

At lunchtime, Natalie sat by herself in a corner of the cafeteria.

"Natalie, you have to tell me what is going on," I said. "What kind of test was it? Is something wrong with you?"

Natalie did not look up. She spoke so softly I could hardly hear her.

"It's my lisp," she whispered. "The speech teacher wants to fix it. I have to go to *speech* class."

Speech class? A lisp? Was that all that was wrong? I was very relieved.

"That isn't so bad," I said.

"It is to me. No one else has to go to speech class," said Natalie.

"What do you do there?" I asked. I thought speech class sounded kind of interesting. I love to make speeches!

"We practice saying 'esses' the right way," replied Natalie. "We make up sentences that have lots of 'S' words. We say the 'S' words while we look in a mirror."

"So you say 'Sally sells seashells at the seashore'? And you look in the mirror while you say it?" I asked. "That sounds like fun."

"It is not fun to be called out of class. It is not fun to have a lisp. And I do not want anyone else to know. So please keep it a secret. Okay?" begged Natalie.

"Okay," I agreed. "I will keep it a secret. I will not tell a soul."

"S" Words

"*I will not tell a soul. I will not tell a soul.*" I repeated the promise over and over to myself until I reached the playground.

Then I changed the promise — just a little. *I will not tell a soul — except for Nancy and Hannie.* I *had* to tell them. They were very worried about Natalie. They thought she was going to the hospital every time she left the room. They thought she was going to see a brain surgeon. They thought maybe she needed an operation.

"*Psst-psst!*" I said. I wanted them to know

I had an important secret to tell them. It was not going to be like saying the Telephone secret out loud. That was a mistake. No, this was different. Nancy and Hannie had to know the truth. It was the only way they would stop worrying. They were the *only* ones I was going to tell. No one else.

"You guys, I have something to tell you," I whispered. "I talked to Natalie. I found out about her tests."

"Tell us!" said Nancy. "Is she going to go to the hospital? Is she going to have an operation?"

"No," I replied. "Natalie is not going to have an operation. She has a lisp. She is going to speech class."

"Speech class! That is good news," said Nancy. "Speech class is not serious at all."

"I never even noticed she has a lisp," said Hannie. "But if she does, I am glad they are fixing it."

"Do you want to know what she does in speech class?" I said. I told Nancy and Hannie all about practicing "S" words in front of a mirror. "She says sentences like, 'Sally sells seashells at the seashore.' "

"Well, I am glad Natalie is not going to have an operation," said Nancy. "Do you want to play hopscotch now?"

"How about tetherball?" suggested Hannie.

I wanted to practice "S" words. But Nancy and Hannie did not seem very interested.

Some kids were already playing tetherball. But the hopscotch court was empty. I took out my special hopscotch stone. I always carry it with me to the playground.

All of a sudden, Hannie said, "Excuse me. I'll be right back!" She ran across the playground. She ran straight to Hank Reubens. I saw her whisper something in his ear.

Hmm. She looked like she was telling him a big secret. I wondered what kind of secret it could be.

I wondered what was going on.

Natalie's Operation

"Hi, Natalie!" I said happily. It was Wednesday morning. I had been feeling happy ever since I found out that Natalie did not have to go to the hospital.

"Hi," mumbled Natalie. She did not sound happy. Wednesday was the day of her speech class. She would have to leave as soon as Ms. Colman had taken attendance.

When she left, you know what happened? Jannie Gilbert burst into tears.

"Jannie, what is wrong?" asked Ms. Colman.

"It's . . . it's awful!" cried Jannie.

"Tell us what is so awful. We will try to help you," said Ms. Colman.

"It's . . . not . . . me. It's . . . Natalie!" said Jannie.

Poor Natalie? Poor *Jannie*! She was sobbing and gulping and hiccuping.

"What about Natalie?" asked Ms. Colman. (Ms. Colman is very patient. That is one of the reasons I like her so much.)

Jannie blew her nose. Then she said to Ms. Colman, "Someone told me Natalie is going to have an operation. Is she going to the hospital soon?" asked Jannie.

"An operation?" said Bobby Gianelli. "I heard she was going to a special eye doctor. I heard she was going blind!"

"She is not going blind," said Hank. "She is going to speech class."

Wait a minute! How did Hank know Natalie was going to speech class? I had not told him.

"Everyone calm down," said Ms. Colman. "Natalie is not going to the hospital for an operation. And she is not going blind."

"Then why does she keep getting called out of the room?" asked Ricky. (I had not told Ricky the secret, either, even though he is my husband.)

"Hank was right," said Ms. Colman. "Natalie has been going to speech class. She has a slight lisp. The speech teacher is helping her correct it. That is all."

"Oh, boy! That's a relief," said Bobby. Sometimes even Bully Bobby can be nice.

"I am glad I told you what was bothering me," said Jannie. "I feel much better now."

The next thing we knew, the door opened. It was Natalie. Everyone stared at her. Her face turned as red as a cherry.

"Hey, Natalie!" called Hank. "How was your speech class?"

"We were all very worried about you," said Jannie.

"We thought you were going to the hospital," said Ricky. "But Ms. Colman told us you go to speech class."

"Hey, I was the one who told everyone about the speech class," said Hank.

"But," said Natalie, "how did *you* know about it, Hank? The only person *I* told was Karen Brewer. And she was not supposed to tell anyone else. She was supposed to keep the secret."

Uh-oh. Suddenly everyone was staring at *me*.

"You Told!"

I passed a note to Natalie. It was a one-word note. It said, "Sorry." But Natalie would not read it.

I faced forward all morning. But I could still feel everyone staring at me. I wanted to turn around so I could wave to Nancy and Hannie. But I did not want to get any meanie looks.

"Sticks and stones will break my bones, but meanie looks will never hurt me." I sang that song to myself three times.

I tried to listen to Ms. Colman. But I could

not. All I could think about was the trouble I was in. It was a long morning.

Lunchtime was awful. When we got to the cafeteria, everyone started yelling at once.

"You've done it again, Blarin' Karen," said Bobby. (I decided Bobby was not nice at all.)

"We thought Natalie was really sick," said Pamela. "It's all your fault!"

"Thanks to you, I spent half my allowance on a fancy get-well card," said Jannie. "I was going to send it to Natalie in the hospital."

The next thing I knew, Natalie was standing right in front of me. We were glasses to glasses and toes to toes.

"You told!" she cried.

Even my husband, Ricky, was mad.

"I am never going to tell you a secret of mine," he said. "Never, ever!"

Only two people were not yelling at me. Nancy was one. Hannie was the other. The Three Musketeers were sticking together.

But practically everyone else was fighting.

"You told me Natalie was going into the hospital!" Jannie shouted at Pamela.

"That is what Terri told *me*," Pamela shouted back.

"That is because Tammy said it to *me*!" shouted Terri.

Then Bobby started yelling at Ricky. "You were the one who said she was going blind!" he yelled.

I closed my eyes. I covered my ears. This was too, too awful!

I wanted to run away and hide. I wanted to get on the Magic School Bus and go to Mars.

"Good-bye, everyone," I shouted.

They were so busy yelling at each other, no one even heard me.

Good Girl, Bad Girl

School was over. Finally. I stood outside with Nancy. We were waiting for Mrs. Dawes to pick us up.

"Do you want to come over to my house?" asked Nancy.

Nancy's house was not exactly Mars. But it was better than going home and thinking about all the trouble I was in.

"Okay," I replied. "Thanks."

"We will do some more good deeds for Mommy. That will make her happy," said Nancy.

As soon as we reached Nancy's house, I called Mommy. She said I could stay there and play. Nancy and I ate a snack. Then we got to work.

We started by polishing the silver. I wiped pink polish all over a round plate. Next, I took a rag and rubbed and rubbed and rubbed. When I finished, the plate was clean and shiny. It was like a mirror. I made funny faces. I made meanie faces. Polishing silver was fun.

"Let's clean the hall closet now," suggested Nancy. "Mommy says it is a mess."

I love cleaning closets. You never know what you are going to find.

We found three umbrellas, one with a yellow duck handle. Quack! Quack!

We found lots of hats. Two rain hats. One straw hat with flowers. A brown wool hat that looked like a pancake. We tried on every one.

I even found my missing green rubber boot.

"Is that yours?" asked Nancy. "I could

never figure out why I had three green boots."

"Now what?" I asked when we finished.

"There's some dirty laundry downstairs. Mommy likes the light things and dark things to be different piles," Nancy replied.

Sorting laundry is not my favorite job. But I wanted to help Nancy do as many good deeds as possible. So we went downstairs. While we were there, Mrs. Dawes came into the basement.

"Girls, I have been watching you work all afternoon. And I just do not understand. Why are you doing this?" she asked.

"We are trying to help you," said Nancy.

"Are you sure that is all? Are you sure you are not in trouble?" asked Mrs. Dawes.

"No," said Nancy. "We are not in trouble."

"Well, I was in a little trouble today at school. But that is not why we are helping you," I said.

"Have you done something wrong? Are

you trying to make up for it?" asked Mrs. Dawes. "I will not be angry with you — as long as you tell the truth."

What a day! No one would listen to me. At school, I told Natalie I was sorry. But she would not listen. And I had just told Mrs. Dawes I was not in trouble. But she would not listen either.

"We are trying to help out before the baby comes," said Nancy.

"Well, thank you," replied Mrs. Dawes. "I just wanted to be sure nothing was wrong."

Mrs. Dawes went back upstairs.

"It does not matter what I do," said Nancy sadly. "If I do something good, Mommy thinks I did something bad. If I do something bad, she won't even get angry."

"Do you want to finish folding the laundry?" I asked.

"Why should we? Mommy does not care if I am good or bad. So I may as well be bad. That will show her," said Nancy.

That sounded like trouble to me.

Karen's Fault

Something was not right. When I arrived at school on Thursday, my friends were talking to each other again. They were finished being mad. Jannie and Pamela were talking to each other. So were Ricky and Bobby. But no one was talking to me.

I heard Bobby say, "Ssh! It's Blarin' Karen. Do not talk to her."

"That's right," said Natalie. "It's all *her* fault.

"Hi, Karen!" said Hannie. At least she was talking to me. Nancy was, too. They were the only ones who were not mad at me — except for Ms. Colman, that is.

"Good morning, class," said our teacher. "Please be seated for attendance." She began calling names. "Karen Brewer."

"Here!" I replied. I wanted to add, "But I wish I were somewhere else." That is because I was sitting between two statues. (Statues do not talk.) The Natalie statue was on one side. The Ricky statue was on the other. (I hoped Ricky and I would not have to get divorced over this.)

"We are going to continue learning about the solar system today," said Ms. Colman. "Karen, you may be the sun."

Oh goody! I thought. The sun is gigundoly important. It is a star. It is the biggest, brightest, and hottest object in the solar system. (That is what it said in the book Ms. Colman read to us.) The kids would not give the silent treatment to the sun. Would they?

They would. And they did. The other kids played the nine planets and the earth's moon. They played a bunch of asteroids. Ms. Colman said they all had to travel around me. But she did not say they had to talk to me. And they didn't. Boo.

At lunchtime, I sat with Hannie and Nancy in the cafeteria.

"You were a great sun," said Hannie. "I should have brought my sunglasses!"

"I was putting on make-believe sun lotion. Did you see?" asked Nancy.

"I saw you!" replied Hannie.

When we finished our lunch, we went outside to the playground. Pamela walked by with Jannie and Leslie.

"*Psst-psst-psst.*" They made believe they were telling secrets to each other. Who cares, I thought? (I cared, that's who.)

The tetherball pole was free. So I played Hannie. I won. Then I played Nancy. I won again. But I could not win another game because no one else would play with me.

After recess, we had art with Mr. Mackey. I am a very talented artist, in case you did not know it. We were making fall collages. We pasted leaves and acorns on colored paper.

"Would you please pass the glue?" I said to Hank.

He passed the glue. But he turned his head in the other direction.

"Thank you very much," I said.

He did not say, "You are welcome." He did not say, "That is an exquisite collage." (He probably would not say "exquisite" even if he was talking to me.) But he was not talking to me. No one was.

It was a yucky day.

Down with Babies

"Do you want to come over to my house again?" asked Nancy.

"Sure!" I replied. School had not been fun. But I knew Nancy's house would be.

Mommy was staying at home with Andrew. (He had a tummy ache.) So Mrs. Dawes drove us home. I called Mommy from Nancy's house. She said I could stay. I told her to please give Andrew a message. "Tell him I hope he feels better," I said. (See what a good big sister I am?)

Nancy and I had apple juice and rice

cakes with peanut butter for our snack. Then we went upstairs to Nancy's room. Pokey was taking a catnap on Nancy's bed.

"Hello, Pokey," I said. I rubbed Pokey behind his ear. I knew he liked it because he started to purr.

"Listen. I have a plan," said Nancy. She looked very serious. "I am not going to let Mommy have this baby."

I stopped rubbing Pokey's ear. I looked at Nancy.

"Why?" I asked.

"I have a new kitten," said Nancy. "I do not need a new baby. And I do not see why Mommy and Daddy need one either."

"I don't think you can stop the baby now," I said.

"Oh, yes, I can," replied Nancy.

"What are you going to do?" I asked.

"I am going to erase Mommy's next doctor's appointment from her calendar. That way she will forget to go. And I am going to hide the suitcase she was going to take to the hospital," said Nancy.

"How will that stop the baby?" I asked.

"It just will," said Nancy. "Help me think of other things to do. And, remember, I can do whatever I want. I'm a *bad* girl now."

I did not like the sound of her plan. But I did not want Nancy to be mad at me. Enough kids were mad at me already. I tried to think of things that would make Nancy feel better, but would not get us into too much trouble.

"We can hide all the new baby books your mommy and daddy bought," I suggested.

"Good idea!" said Nancy. We ran downstairs. There was a pile of books in the living room. We hid them in the back of the closet we had cleaned.

"Okay! We're done," I said. "Now let's make Pokey a rubber band ball. That would be fun." (I was not having fun yet at Nancy's house.)

"No," said Nancy firmly. "We are not

THE TRUTH ABOUT PARENTING

WHAT EVERY PARENT SHOULD KNOW

MOST OF
WHAT YOU'VE ALWAYS
WANTED TO KNOW ABOUT BABIES

THE FIRST TWELVE MONTHS

PARENTING WITHOUT TEARS

HAVING a BABY

YOU and YOUR BABY

RAISING YOUR CHILD

finished yet. I have another idea. Let's move some old chairs and things into the guest room. We will fill it up so it cannot be the baby's room anymore."

"Won't that make a lot of noise?" I asked.

"It's okay. Mommy is way downstairs in the basement doing the laundry. She won't hear us," said Nancy.

We moved three chairs, a small table, and an old trunk into the guest room. By the time we finished there was no room for a crib. There was not even room for a rag doll.

"Want to help me hide Mommy's suitcase now?" asked Nancy.

"I do not think so. I better go home and keep Andrew company," I said. "I'll see you tomorrow."

"Okay, 'bye," said Nancy. But she wasn't paying any attention to me. She was busy dragging her mommy's suitcase out from under the bed.

Nancy was down on babies.

"I Have A Secret"

Psst-psst, psst-psst, psst-psst-psst. It was Friday morning. As soon as I came into my classroom, the kids started whispering to each other.

Oh, no, I thought. Not another day of the silent treatment.

Then Bobby said to me, "I have a secret, Blarin' Karen . . . but I am not telling it to *you*."

"You don't have to!" I replied happily. Bobby was being a meanie. But at least he was talking to me.

"Have you blabbed any secrets yet today?" asked Leslie.

"No, but it's still early," I replied. I felt very relieved. Two kids had spoken to me. Today was going to be much better than yesterday.

I went to the back of the room to talk to Nancy and Hannie before Ms. Colman arrived. On the way, I passed Pamela and Jannie.

"Could you walk a little faster, please?" said Pamela. "We don't want you to hear what we are saying."

"That's right," said Jannie. "If we wanted the whole class to know what we were saying, we would tell them ourselves."

"Don't worry," I said. "I am not interested in your secrets."

I passed Terri and Tammy next. They lowered their voices to a whisper when they saw me. I kept on walking.

"Hi, Hannie. Hi, Nancy," I said.

"Guess what I did after you left my house," said Nancy. "I hid Mommy's suitcase. I erased the doctor's appointment from her calendar. And I threw away all the baby food and diaper coupons she and Daddy have been saving."

"I do not think that is going to stop the baby from coming," said Hannie.

"Me neither," I agreed.

"Good morning, class," said Ms. Colman. "It's time to start our day."

I leaned over to Nancy and Hannie and whispered, "See you later."

"Why are we whispering?" whispered Nancy.

"If everyone else in this room can have secrets, so can we," I replied.

"Right," whispered Hannie. "See you later."

After attendance Natalie was called over the P.A. system.

"See you later, Natalie!" called Pamela.

"You can look at my notebook when you come back," said Bobby.

I was glad everyone was being nice to Natalie. No one teased her at all about speech class. That is what she had been afraid of in the first place. That is why she had wanted me to keep her speech classes a secret.

So that was okay — even if Natalie's secret wasn't a secret anymore. Now I just had to get myself out of trouble. I was tired of hearing *psst-psst-psst*. I was tired of everyone keeping secrets. I had to do something. And I knew what that something was going to be.

I was going to apologize to Natalie. I was going to make a public announcement. I wanted everyone to hear me.

"Say You're Sorry"

"I have made an important decision," I announced to Nancy and Hannie. We were in the cafeteria eating lunch. It was hard to sound important with a mouthful of peanut butter sandwich. So I swallowed some milk to wash it down. Then I continued.

"I am going to apologize to Natalie. And I want to do it in front of everyone," I said.

Nancy and Hannie thought that was a good idea.

"Why don't you do it right now?" suggested Hannie. "You can do it on the playground."

"Okay," I said. "I will."

Our classmates were starting to leave the cafeteria, I had to act fast. I jumped up and said in my biggest outdoor voice (even though we were still indoors), "Attention, everybody! I have something to say to Natalie. If you would like to hear what it is, meet me outside on the playground."

There. That was done. Next I had to think of just what to say. I took one last swallow of my milk.

"Do I have a milk mustache?" I asked Nancy.

"A little one on the left side," she replied.

I wiped my mouth with the back of my hand. I did not want to have a milk mustache when I made my announcement. I did not want to look like a dweeb.

I walked outside and stood under a tree on the playground. When I turned around, everyone in my class was facing me. My apology was not quite ready. I thought quickly. *Greetings, fellow classmates*. No, that was no good. I tried again. *Natalie, dear friend, who sits in the front row with me . . .*

I realized Hannie was nudging me. "Go ahead, Karen. Say you're sorry," she whispered.

Why didn't I think of that? I wondered. I took a deep breath. The words began pouring out of my mouth.

"Natalie, I am very sorry," I said. "I should have kept your secret. You trusted me and I let you down."

That was probably enough. I wanted to say one more thing.

"I would also like to point out that I was not the only person who could not keep a secret. I only told one person. I did not tell the whole class. So how did the whole class find out? They found out because everybody else told just one person, too. I am not the only one who cannot keep a secret," I said.

Maybe that was enough. But I thought

of one more thing I wanted to say.

"The last thing I want to say is this. The only reason I told the secret in the first place was because I was very worried about you, Natalie. I did not do it to be mean."

There. My speech was finished. I thought it was pretty good. I took a bow.

"I accept your apology, Karen," said Natalie. "Maybe I should not have made such a big deal about keeping my speech classes a secret. Maybe I should have told the truth to begin with. If I had told the truth, none of this would have happened."

"I'm sorry I did not keep the secret, too, Karen," said Nancy. "I told it to Hannie."

"And I told Hank," Hannie admitted.

"I told the secret to Bobby," said Ricky. "I'm sorry, Karen and Natalie."

By the time recess was over, everyone had said they were sorry to everyone else. The fight was over.

The Truth

School was over. Nancy and I were in her room. We were playing with Pokey. Nancy promised me that we would not have to hide any more baby things.

"I wish you had been with us at school today, Pokey," I said. "You would have been very proud of me."

"*I* was proud of you. You told the truth to everyone," said Nancy.

"Thanks," I replied. "I decided to come clean and confess."

"Well, I am going to come clean and confess, too," said Nancy. "I am going to tell Mommy about everything."

"I think that's a good idea. I will go with you," I said. "After all, I helped you."

"Okay," said Nancy. "We'll do it now."

"Pokey, you can stay here," I said. "You are innocent."

Mrs. Dawes was in the kitchen. She was on the phone. She did not look very happy.

"I am so sorry," she said. "I usually do not forget my appointments. Can we make it next Friday instead?"

Nancy and I looked at each other. I knew we were both wondering the same thing. Was this the best time to tell the truth?

Mrs. Dawes hung up the phone. We had to decide fast.

"Hello, girls," she said. Then she sighed. "Can I get you something?"

"No, thank you, Mommy," said Nancy. She looked at me. I nodded. It was now or never.

"We . . . we have something to tell you," said Nancy.

"I'm listening," replied Mrs. Dawes.

"It's about your doctor's appointment. It's about why you missed it," said Nancy.

"It was our fault, Mrs. Dawes," I said. "We did some things the other day so you wouldn't have the baby. We hid your baby books and moved furniture into the guest room and . . ."

"And I erased your doctor's appointment from your calendar!" Nancy blurted out.

"Oh, girls! How *could* you?" cried Mrs. Dawes in a loud voice. It was not an outdoor voice. It was more like an angry voice.

"We are very, very sorry," I said. (This was my day for "I am sorry" speeches.)

"Karen, I would appreciate it if you went home now. I would like to talk with Nancy."

"Okay, I understand. 'Bye, Nancy," I said. I walked out the door. I did not go very far. There was something I needed to tell Nancy. I poked my head back inside.

"Tell your mother *why* you do not want her to have the baby," I said. "Tell her the whole story. Tell her the *truth.*"

Nancy and Her Mother

"I'm so sorry, Mommy," sobbed Nancy. "I did all those things because I was worried about having a new brother or sister."

I was still standing there. I hoped Nancy and her mother would not mind.

"What are you worried about? Can you tell me?" asked Mrs. Dawes.

"I am worried about what will happen to *me*. I am afraid that the baby is going to be smarter than me. Or better at doing things. Then you and Daddy won't love me anymore," said Nancy.

"Time for a talk," said Mrs. Dawes. She pulled Nancy into her lap.

"Ahem," I said.

"You may stay," said Mrs. Dawes.

"Thanks," I said. I pulled up a chair.

"Nancy, I am going to tell you something I hope you won't ever forget. If you do, I will remind you: You are very special to Daddy and me. Nothing and no one can change that. No baby — no matter how wonderful — can take your place."

Nancy gave her mommy a big hug.

"We will love your baby brother or sister. But parents can love their children differently," explained Mrs. Dawes. "Your daddy and I have a lot of love to give. And we are not going to love you any less when the baby comes. Do you understand?"

"Yes," Nancy replied.

"Are you *sure*?" asked Mrs. Dawes.

Nancy nodded her head.

"I understand, too!" I cried. "I am a big sister *and* a little sister. Once I was worried that Daddy loved Emily Michelle more than

me. But that was not so. He said the same things you did. And now I know they are true."

There it was again. The truth. I was glad we had told Mrs. Dawes the truth about the things we did. And I was glad that Nancy's worries about the new baby were not a secret anymore.

"I really am sorry I erased your appointment," said Nancy.

"And I am sorry we hid the baby books. I'll go get them!" I offered.

"I will get your suitcase," said Nancy, climbing off her mother's lap.

"And we will move the furniture back where it came from," I added.

"That would be nice," said Mrs. Dawes.

"But we will not put the dust back in the living room. And we will not put the leaves back on the lawn," I promised.

"See? We did some good things," said Nancy.

"You do a lot of good things," said Mrs. Dawes. "But you know what? I would love you even if you didn't."

"Say Your 'Esses'"

It was another rainy day recess. Ms. Colman was organizing our indoor games.

"Hey, Karen!" yelled Bobby. "Want to play Telephone?"

Bobby was teasing me. But I did not care.

"Sure," I replied. "I'll play!"

I heard Pamela say to Leslie, "Do you still want to play? Even if Karen does?"

"I don't know," said Leslie. "Some people cannot keep secrets no matter how hard they try."

I can keep a secret, I thought. I know I can. I'll show everyone.

We picked numbers from the box on Ms. Colman's desk. Natalie got number one. I got number five. Ms. Colman wrote a secret sentence on a piece of paper. She handed it to Natalie.

Psst-psst-psst-psst. Natalie whispered to Bobby. Bobby whispered to Pamela. Pamela whispered to Ricky. Ricky whispered to me.

As soon as the secret went into my ear, I covered my mouth so the secret would not pop out.

"Wait," said Bobby. "I will get you a needle and thread. You can sew your lips together."

I could tell he was being funny. Not mean.

"Careful, Karen," warned Pamela. "Don't let that secret slip out."

"Mmph-mmph, mmph-mmph" I mumbled. That meant "My lips are sealed."

I turned to Hannie and uncovered my

mouth. Then I stopped and slapped my forehead.

"Oh, no!" I said out loud. "I forgot the sentence!"

"Ka-ren!" moaned Natalie.

"Just kidding!" I replied. I turned to Hannie and whispered the secret. *Psst-psst-psst-psst.*

"She did it!" cried Ricky. "She kept the secret."

Everyone clapped and cheered for me, Karen Brewer, Great Keeper of the Telephone Secret.

The secret went down the line until it reached Nancy. She was the last player.

"Okay. Here it is," said Nancy. *"Wayne, Wayne, go way, way. Gum again a nut today!"*

"Oh, no!" giggled Natalie. "That was not how it started out at all."

She read what Ms. Colman had written. *"Rain, rain, go away. Come again another day."*

"That game was fun!" said Hannie.

"I have an idea for a new game," said Natalie. "It is called Speech Class. Who wants to play?"

"I do!" I cried. Nancy, Hannie, and a few other kids wanted to play, too.

"May we borrow your mirror, Ms. Colman?" asked Natalie.

"Of course," Ms. Colman replied. She handed Natalie a mirror from her desk drawer.

"Thank you," said Natalie. "Okay, everyone. We are going to take turns saying our 'esses' while we look in the mirror. Karen, will you begin?"

I looked in the mirror and began to say my "esses." I could see Natalie's face behind me. She was smiling.

I could tell she was glad her speech classes were not a secret anymore. Just like Nancy was glad when her worries about the baby were not a secret anymore. Do you want to know what I think?

I think some secrets are better when they are shared.

About the Author

ANN M. MARTIN lives in New York City and loves animals, especially cats. She has two cats of her own, Mouse and Rosie.

Other books by Ann M. Martin that you might enjoy are *Stage Fright*; *Me and Katie (the Pest)*; and the books in *The Baby-sitters Club* series.

Ann likes ice cream and *I Love Lucy*. And she has her own little sister, whose name is Jane.

Little Sister

Don't miss #34

KAREN'S SNOW DAY

That night I was too excited to fall asleep.

"Bedtime, Karen!" called Mommy.

"Okay," I replied. But when she and Seth came into my room, I was jumping up and down on my bed. "I *love* storms!" I announced.

"Settle down, honey," said Seth.

I tried to. But after I turned out my light, I kept sitting up to look out the window. Once the snow was coming down so hard I could not even see the house across the street.

I woke up early on Thursday morning. I tuned into Dr. G. I knew school would be closed, but I wanted to hear Dr. G. say so himself. When he said, "In Stoneybrook, all public, private, and parochial schools are closed," I cheered. "Yeah! Hooray!"

LITTLE APPLE®

BABY SITTERS Little Sister™

by Ann M. Martin,
author of The Baby-sitters Club ®

☐	MQ44300-3	#1	Karen's Witch	$2.95
☐	MQ44259-7	#2	Karen's Roller Skates	$2.95
☐	MQ44299-7	#3	Karen's Worst Day	$2.95
☐	MQ44264-3	#4	Karen's Kittycat Club	$2.95
☐	MQ44258-9	#5	Karen's School Picture	$2.95
☐	MQ44298-8	#6	Karen's Little Sister	$2.95
☐	MQ44257-0	#7	Karen's Birthday	$2.95
☐	MQ42670-2	#8	Karen's Haircut	$2.95
☐	MQ43652-X	#9	Karen's Sleepover	$2.95
☐	MQ43651-1	#10	Karen's Grandmothers	$2.95
☐	MQ43650-3	#11	Karen's Prize	$2.95
☐	MQ43649-X	#12	Karen's Ghost	$2.95
☐	MQ43648-1	#13	Karen's Surprise	$2.95
☐	MQ43646-5	#14	Karen's New Year	$2.95
☐	MQ43645-7	#15	Karen's in Love	$2.95
☐	MQ43644-9	#16	Karen's Goldfish	$2.95
☐	MQ43643-0	#17	Karen's Brothers	$2.95
☐	MQ43642-2	#18	Karen's Home-Run	$2.75
☐	MQ43641-4	#19	Karen's Good-Bye	$2.95
☐	MQ44823-4	#20	Karen's Carnival	$2.95
☐	MQ44824-2	#21	Karen's New Teacher	$2.95
☐	MQ44833-1	#22	Karen's Little Witch	$2.95
☐	MQ44832-3	#23	Karen's Doll	$2.95
☐	MQ44859-5	#24	Karen's School Trip	$2.95
☐	MQ44831-5	#25	Karen's Pen Pal	$2.95
☐	MQ44830-7	#26	Karen's Ducklings	$2.95
☐	MQ44829-3	#27	Karen's Big Joke	$2.95
☐	MQ44828-5	#28	Karen's Tea Party	$2.95
☐	MQ44825-0	#29	Karen's Cartwheel	$2.75
☐	MQ45645-8	#30	Karen's Kittens	$2.95
☐	MQ45646-6	#31	Karen's Bully	$2.95
☐	MQ45647-4	#32	Karen's Pumpkin Patch	$2.95
☐	MQ45648-2	#33	Karen's Secret	$2.95
☐	MQ45650-4	#34	Karen's Snow Day	$2.95
☐	MQ45652-0	#35	Karen's Doll Hospital	$2.95
☐	MQ45651-2	#36	Karen's New Friend	$2.95
☐	MQ45653-9	#37	Karen's Tuba	$2.95
☐	MQ45655-5	#38	Karen's Big Lie	$2.95
☐	MQ45654-7	#39	Karen's Wedding	$2.95
☐	MQ47040-X	#40	Karen's Newspaper	$2.95
☐	MQ47041-8	#41	Karen's School	$2.95
☐	MQ47042-6	#42	Karen's Pizza Party	$2.95
☐	MQ46912-6	#43	Karen's Toothache	$2.95

More Titles... ➡

♥ ♥

♥ *The Baby-sitters Little Sister titles continued...*

♥ □	MQ47043-4	#44	Karen's Big Weekend	$2.95
□	MQ47044-2	#45	Karen's Twin	$2.95
□	MQ47045-0	#46	Karen's Baby-sitter	$2.95
□	MQ46913-4	#47	Karen's Kite	$2.95
□	MQ47046-9	#48	Karen's Two Families	$2.95
□	MQ47047-7	#49	Karen's Stepmother	$2.95
□	MQ47048-5	#50	Karen's Lucky Penny	$2.95
□	MQ48229-7	#51	Karen's Big Top	$2.95
□	MQ48299-8	#52	Karen's Mermaid	$2.95
□	MQ48300-5	#53	Karen's School Bus	$2.95
□	MQ48301-3	#54	Karen's Candy	$2.95
□	MQ48230-0	#55	Karen's Magician	$2.95
□	MQ48302-1	#56	Karen's Ice Skates	$2.95
□	MQ48303-X	#57	Karen's School Mystery	$2.95
□	MQ48304-8	#58	Karen's Ski Trip	$2.95
□	MQ48231-9	#59	Karen's Leprechaun	$2.95
□	MQ48305-6	#60	Karen's Pony	$2.95
□	MQ48306-4	#61	Karen's Tattletale	$2.95
□	MQ48307-2	#62	Karen's New Bike	$2.95
□	MQ25996-2	#63	Karen's Movie	$2.95
□	MQ25997-0	#64	Karen's Lemonade Stand	$2.95
□	MQ25998-9	#65	Karen's Toys	$2.95
□	MQ26279-3	#66	Karen's Monsters	$2.95
□	MQ26024-3	#67	Karen's Turkey Day	$2.95
□	MQ26025-1	#68	Karen's Angel	$2.95
□	MQ26193-2	#69	Karen's Big Sister	$2.95
□	MQ26280-7	#70	Karen's Grandad	$2.95
□	MQ26194-0	#71	Karen's Island Adventure	$2.95
□	MQ26195-9	#72	Karen's New Puppy	$2.95
□	MQ55407-7		BSLS Jump Rope Rhymes Pack	$5.99
□	MQ47677-7		BSLS School Scrapbook	$2.95
□	MQ43647-3		Karen's Wish Super Special #1	$3.25
□	MQ44834-X		Karen's Plane Trip Super Special #2	$3.25
□	MQ44827-7		Karen's Mystery Super Special #3	$3.25
□	MQ45644-X		Karen, Hannie, and Nancy — The Three Musketeers Super Special #4	$2.95
□	MQ45649-0		Karen's Baby Super Special #5	$3.50
□	MQ46911-8		Karen's Campout Super Special #6	$3.25

♥ Available wherever you buy books, or use this order form.

- -

Scholastic Inc., P.O. Box 7502, 2931 E. McCarty Street, Jefferson City, MO 65102

Please send me the books I have checked above. I am enclosing $ _____ (please add $2.00 to cover shipping and handling). Send check or money order – no cash or C.O.Ds please.

♥ Name _____ Birthdate _____

♥ Address _____

♥ City _____ State/Zip _____

Please allow four to six weeks for delivery. Offer good in U.S.A. only. Sorry, mail orders are not available to residents to Canada. Prices subject to change.   BLS995

♥ ♥

LITTLE  APPLE®

*T*here are fun times ahead with kids just like you in Little Apple books! Once you take a bite out of a Little Apple—you'll want to read more!

Reading Excitement for Kids with BIG Appetites!

- ❏ NA42833-0 **Catwings** Ursula K. LeGuin $2.95
- ❏ NA42832-2 **Catwings Return** Ursula K. LeGuin $2.95
- ❏ NA41821-1 **Class Clown** Johanna Hurwitz $2.75
- ❏ NA43868-9 **The Haunting of Grade Three**
  Grace Maccarone $2.75
- ❏ NA40966-2 **Rent A Third Grader** B.B. Hiller $2.99
- ❏ NA41944-7 **The Return of the Third Grade Ghost Hunters**
  Grace Maccarone $2.75
- ❏ NA44477-8 **Santa Claus Doesn't Mop Floors**
  Debra Dadey and Marcia Thornton Jones $2.99
- ❏ NA42031-3 **Teacher's Pet** Johanna Hurwitz $2.99
- ❏ NA43411-X **Vampires Don't Wear Polka Dots**
  Debra Dadey and Marcia Thornton Jones $2.99
- ❏ NA44061-6 **Werewolves Don't Go to Summer Camp**
  Debra Dadey and Marcia Thornton Jones $2.99

Available wherever you buy books...or use the coupon below.

SCHOLASTIC INC., Box 7502, 2931 East McCarty Street, Jefferson City, MO 65102

Please send me the books I have checked above. I am enclosing $ _____ (please add $2.00 to cover shipping and handling). Send check or money order—no cash or C.O.D.s please.

Name _____

Address _____

City _____ State/Zip _____

Please allow four to six weeks for delivery. Offer good in the U.S.A. only. Sorry, mail orders are not available to residents of Canada. Prices subject to change.

LA595